RESCUE BOATS

BY LORI DITTMER

CREATIVE EDUCATION • CREATIVE PAPERBACKS

Published by Creative Education and Creative Paperbacks
P.O. Box 227, Mankato, Minnesota 56002
Creative Education and Creative Paperbacks are imprints of
The Creative Company
www.thecreativecompany.us

Design by The Design Lab
Production by Dana Cheit
Art direction by Rita Marshall
Printed in the United States of America

Photographs by Alamy (Paul Bock, DBURKE, David Osborn),
Dreamstime (Fotomicar, Seagames50, Egon Zitter), Getty Images
(Rick Friedman/Corbis Historical), iStockphoto (Andyteight, ilbusca,
nicolamargaret, Photobos), Shutterstock (daseaford, deepspace,
Scanrail1, silvergull)

Library of Congress Cataloging-in-Publication Data
Names: Dittmer, Lori, author.
Title: Rescue boats / Lori Dittmer.
Series: Amazing rescue vehicles.
Includes bibliographical references and index.
Summary: A basic exploration of the parts, equipment, and varia-
tions of rescue boats, the nautical rescue vehicles. Also included is a
pictorial diagram of the important rescue vehicle and its equipment.
Identifiers: ISBN 978-1-64026-044-3 (hardcover) / ISBN 978-1-
62832-632-1 (pbk) / ISBN 978-1-64000-160-2 (eBook)
This title has been submitted for CIP processing under LCCN
2018938945.

CCSS: RI.1.1, 2, 4, 5, 6, 7; RI.2.2, 5, 6, 7, 10; RI.3.1, 5, 7, 8;
RF.1.1, 3, 4; RF.2.3, 4

First Edition HC 9 8 7 6 5 4 3 2 1
First Edition PBK 9 8 7 6 5 4 3 2 1

Table of Contents

In the 1900s, wooden rescue boats began to be powered by motors.

Rescue boats search for people in trouble. They **navigate** rivers and lakes. They patrol coastlines and **open water**. Early rescue boats were made of wood. Volunteers rowed them with oars.

navigate to travel using a planned route

open water water that is not surrounded by land or ice

Boats with air-filled hulls are known as Zodiacs.

Today, most rescue boats have engines. Some have a **hull** that is filled with air. Others have hard, or rigid, hulls. Still others use a combination.

hull the main body of a ship, including the bottom, sides, and deck

Small rescue boats might carry just two crew members. They help people in rivers or flooded areas. These flat-bottomed boats move through shallow water without getting stuck. They can search close to shore, too.

Rescue equipment is tied down so that it does not get in the way.

A lookout watches for anything that could come into the boat's path.

Larger boats have **wheelhouses**. They hold many crew members. These boats go farther out to sea. They can handle rough waves and bad weather. Large rescue boats might even carry smaller boats with them.

wheelhouses enclosed areas on a boat or ship where a person stands to steer

The crew uses a radio to talk to ships in trouble. They also talk to other rescue vehicles. **Radar** and **sonar** equipment show where boats or people are in the water.

radar a device used to determine the direction, distance, and speed of objects

sonar a device used to determine the location of objects, especially underwater

Crew members know how to safely pull a person out of the water.

A coxswain steers the boat. Other crew members are trained to deal with **emergencies**. They might need to enter the water to save someone. They give **first aid** to those who are hurt.

coxswain the person who steers a boat and is in charge of its crew

emergencies unexpected, dangerous situations that require immediate action

first aid help given to a sick or injured person until full medical aid is available

Rescue boats work with other rescue vehicles. Helicopters help them search for people who are stranded. They pull them from the water. Or they help them escape a sinking ship. Rescue boats carry supplies like blankets and food.

Helicopters may take the injured from a rescue boat to a hospital.

Some rescue boats fight fires. They pump water straight from the ocean. Then they spray it on the fire. Icebreakers ram through ice to free ships that are trapped.

Fireboats have powerful pumps that shoot water onto the fire.

Rescue boats save lives. If you see one speeding through the water, think about the amazing work it does!

Rescue boats patrol coastlines and open water to make sure people are safe.

Rescue Boat Blueprint

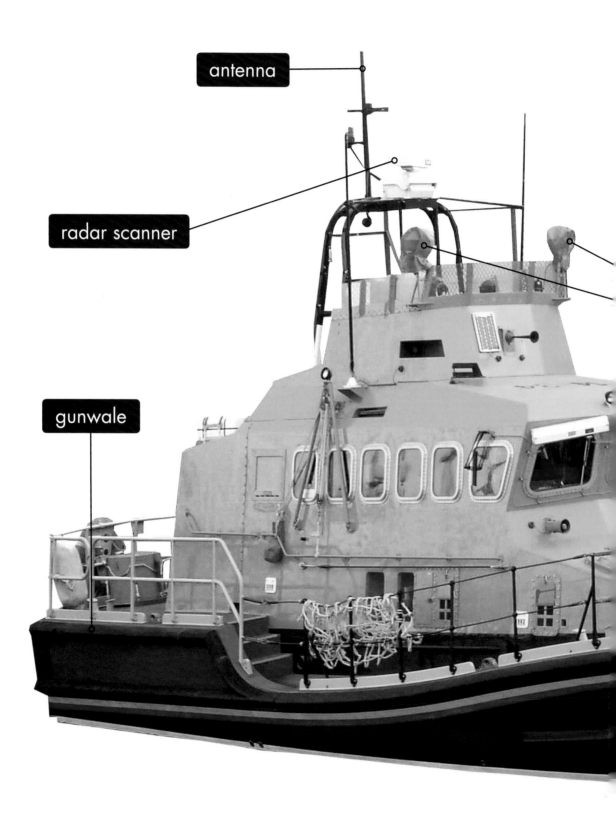

antenna

radar scanner

gunwale

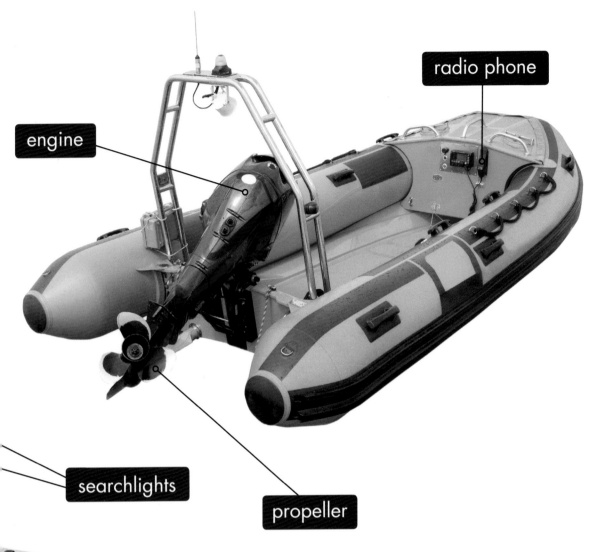

engine

radio phone

searchlights

propeller

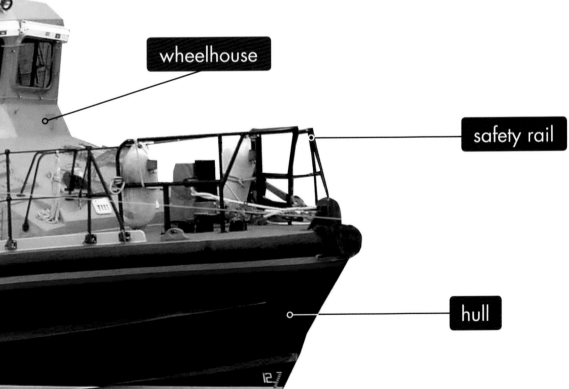

wheelhouse

safety rail

hull

Read More

Fortuna, Lois. *Rescue Boats*. New York: Gareth Stevens, 2016.

Oxlade, Chris. *Rescue Boat*. Mankato, Minn.: QEB, 2010.

Websites

Lifeboats for Children: Gecko's Real Vehicles
https://www.youtube.com/watch?v=nO1uRoqXxd4
Watch a video about a lifeboat, and see the crew practice a rescue.

United States Coast Guard: The Official Coast Guard Coloring Book
https://www.uscg.mil/Community-Relations/Coast-Guard-Coloring-Book/
Read about the U.S. Coast Guard, and print out the pages to color.

Note: Every effort has been made to ensure that the websites listed above are suitable for children, that they have educational value, and that they contain no inappropriate material. However, because of the nature of the Internet, it is impossible to guarantee that these sites will remain active indefinitely or that their contents will not be altered.

Index